THE ADVENTURES OF

LEILA
THE
FAIRY
PRINCESS

Roger McIntosh and Leila McGrath

Ackroyd House

Cliffe Lane

Cleckheaton

BD194ET

This book is dedicated to my granddaughter Leila, whose creative enthusiasm and vivid imagination inspired me to change my writing genre and write a children's book.

The concept first came to light when we were sat in a well known coffee shop after taking her to a school cross country run.

I ordered my usual extra hot, extra shot, short cappuccino and she ordered a hot chocolate with whipped cream and chocolate sprinkles.

Now it might have been the adrenaline from just doing a cross country run or the sugar content of the hot chocolate but Leila started talking enthusiastically about a fairy she dreamed about that visited children's

gardens.

After slowing her down a little so I could keep up with

her energy and understand the concept, I asked her did

she write any of it down. Her answer was no but she

told her mother about it and she said she would write it

down for her.

When I spoke to my daughter as other busy mothers

may testify, she couldn't really remember the story and

didn't have time to write it down.

"You're a writer, " she said. "Can you write a book for

her? Although I had 2 other books on the go, I decided

to change my whole writing genre and try my first

children's book.

"I now have to thank my daughter and my granddaughter, because writing this book has made me open up my own childish mind again and experience the wonders of imagination where anything can happen.

CONTENT

CHAPTER 1

Sad Sarah

In a magical forest far, far away, the tiny residents go about their daily lives spreading love and magic, making it a better place for everyone. The forest is a wondrous and enchanting place, where the trees stand so tall and majestic that they seem to pierce the deep blue sky. The air is fresh and clean, filled with the sweet scent of wildflowers and evergreens. As you enter the forest, soft glowing fireflies twinkle and dance around the trees, leading you deeper and deeper into this enchanting place. Bright green luscious grass carpets the forest floor and cushions your feet as you walk, while a rainbow of beautiful flowers sway in the cool breeze as if dancing to silent music.

Along the many winding paths, you will discover hidden clearings filled with mystical creatures such as: Fairies, Pixies, Unicorns and Centaurs, all happily going about their individual duties. The fairies with their delicate features and magical powers, rule the village and are lead by a King and Queen who have four children, Leila, Luca, little Lois and baby Luna. The pixies with their pointed ears, expressive eyes and mischievous ways, sing along as they work to help the fairies keep the forest clean. White unicorns with their single spiralled horn, gallop around; flowing manes and tails wafting majestically in the wind. The half man, half horse Centaurs protect the inhabitants of the village from danger, wielding their bows and arrows as a warning to those who may want to cause them harm.

The trees in this magical forest are unlike any you've ever seen before. They are decorated with colourful leaves and the trunks are covered in vines and moss that glow with a luminous light at night. The branches reach out like arms, creating a canopy overhead that filters the sunlight, casting a soft and warm glow over the forest floor.

The forest is always alive with the sound of birds singing, waterfalls trickling and the rustling of leaves as the many animals that inhabit this place forage for food. If you listen carefully you can usually hear the distant sound of laughter and music, signalling the presence of a nearby gathering of pixie's.

As the day begins to draw to a close, the forest transforms once again as the sky darkens and the fireflies glow brighter, creating an even more magical and mysterious spectacle.

Magical Forest

Other glowing creatures emerge from the shadows and the stars twinkle overhead creating a wondrous atmosphere and magnificent light show. In this magical forest, time appears to stand still and the worries of the outside world seem to fade away as the residents enjoy its peace and tranquility. This is a place of pure wonder and delight, where anything can happen and everything is possible.

One of the residents of this forest is a beautiful fairy Princess called Leila. She is not just known for her extraordinary magical powers but also her enchanting personality. Although she is small in height, she has a huge heart and lots of courage that would challenge even the biggest of creatures! Her delicate wings change colour to match her many outfits. Her long, flowing golden hair is sometimes adorned with a royal tiara which she doesn't like to wear because it is really heavy and makes her head itch. Her eyes sparkle with magic and her voice is so soft and sweet that it sounds like somebody is playing a harp.

She is the daughter of King Jamie and Queen Melissa who rule over the fairy village. Her younger brother Prince Luca is head of the village army and has a troop of centaurs who help to keep the villagers safe. Although Leila is older than her brother, the rule is that the kingdom of the village goes to the male of the family so Luca is next in line to be King. Leila isn't bothered though, she doesn't want all the fuss of being the Queen of the village. She much prefers to spend her days playing with her friends in the forest and helping to make children around the forest happy.

Leila has the ability to grant wishes and her powers are only limited by the imaginations of those who seek her help. She appears in times of great need, offering guidance and assistance to both children and animals alike.

Leila

She is one of the guardians of the forest where she lives and takes her job very seriously. Despite her many powers and her royal family background, she is a humble and kind-hearted fairy, with a very generous nature. She is admired by all of the other fairies and pixies in the village and her name is always spoken with respect by all who know her.

Leila loves her job as a fairy and much prefers spending her days helping people than being a princess stuck in the village. She is always on the look out for those who need her help and feels every child has the right to be loved and happy. Whenever she finds a child who is sad or lonely, she visits them and tries her best to help them out by waving her wand and granting them their wishes.

One day, Leila meets a little girl, who is sitting under a tree crying.

"Oh dear, whatever is the matter?" she asks gently, but the little girl just carries on crying. Leila tries again, but this time a little louder.

"Why are you crying, can I help you?" she asks. The girl looks up for the first time and is shocked to see a fairy at the bottom of her garden but Leila has such a kind and friendly face that she soon relaxes and isn't afraid.

"It's Lulu, my doll, I can't find her anywhere," she says starting to cry again.

"Now, now, that's enough of that," Leila says kindly, producing a tissue from thin air and giving it to her.

"What's your name?" she asks.

"Sarah," replies the girl.

"Well Sarah, my name is Leila and I am going to help you find your doll," she says confidently.

"Now wipe your eyes and tell me when you last saw her?"

Sarah does what she is told and wipes her tears before answering Leila's question.

"I was playing with her in the garden over there and my mother called me in to have some dinner so I put her under that tree and now she is gone," says the girl getting sadder and sadder and tears rolling down her cheeks again.

"And what does this doll look like?" asks Leila, like a detective solving a case.

"She is a rag doll with black hair that I put in a ponytail and she is wearing a sparkly gold dress," says Sarah.

Sarah

Leila thinks for a while then waves her magic wand and says:

"Bididy bobidy boo," making a beautiful bumble bee with yellow and black stripes appear.

"Hi Bertie," she says to the bee.

"Sarah here has lost her favourite doll somewhere in this garden, can you please help us to look for it?"

"Yes, no problem Leila, I will have a look around and let you know if I find anything," buzzes Bertie in such a gentle whisper that Sarah could hardly hear him speak.

The doll had been given to Sarah when she was a baby and she has slept with it every night since so it really means a lot to her. Leila and Sarah hunt around the garden looking for the doll. The search is also joined by a passing red and black butterfly called Brenda who sees the commotion and wants to help.

They look under the garden bench, in the bushes and even in the neighbours garden but they can't find it anywhere.

After a while Bertie returns and whispers something in Leila's ear.

Bertie

"Great news everybody, Bertie has found Sarah's doll," Leila announces.

"Where is it?" asks Sarah excitedly.

Leila points to the sky.

"Come on you, bring it down," she commands. Everybody looks up and squints at the sun lit sky, trying to see where she is pointing. After a few seconds they see a black and white magpie emerging from a single white cloud. It flies down dropping Sarah's doll at their feet.

"And what have you got to say for yourself Maggie?" asks Leila, to the bird in a stern voice. The magpie sheepishly walks slowly over to Leila with her head down.

"Sorry," squaws Maggie.

"I was flying over the garden and the beautiful sparkly dress caught my eye and I couldn't resist the temptation to pick it up. I didn't realise that it belonged to Sarah. I thought it would look great in my nest because I don't have anything or anybody to play with. All the other magpies are in pairs and sometimes I get lonely by myself. It wasn't until Bertie told me how upset Sarah was that I realised what I had done. I didn't mean to cause any pain or sadness."

Leila although not happy with her taking the doll, noticed the sincerity in Maggie's voice and the remorse in her eyes. She takes a deep breath and speaks softly,

"Maggie, what you did was wrong, but I can see that you genuinely regret it. The doll is indeed special to Sarah, this can be a lesson for you to learn from."

Maggie listens intently as Leila continues.

Maggie

"Remember it is important to seek permission before taking something that doesn't belong to you. We all have treasures in our lives and respecting other peoples things is a quality we must value."

Moved by her forgiving words, Maggie promises to be more considerate and thoughtful in the future. She vows to learn from this mistake and carry the lesson in her heart for all time. Sarah is also touched by Maggie's sincerity and offers to play with her in the garden whenever she feels lonely.

From that day forward, Maggie never took anything without asking permission because she understood the value of seeking consent, recognising that every possession holds meaning to its owner. Sarah is so happy to have her doll back and thanks Leila, Bertie and Brenda for their help.

"How can I ever repay you?" Sarah asks.

"I don't need anything in return, just seeing you happy is reward enough for me," says Leila.

From that day on, Sarah and Leila became the best of friends. Leila would visit her at the bottom of her garden and they would talk, play games and sing songs. The more Leila visited Sarah, the more the garden and Sarah blossomed until the time came when Sarah and the garden were both mature enough that they didn't need Leila anymore. That is always the saddest part for Leila but a good sign that she has done her job well and it is time for her to move on and help other children.

CHAPTER 2

Lost Daisy

In this beautiful enchanting forest lives a young deer named Daisy. Daisy is a curious and adventurous deer, always eager to explore the world around her but sometimes, her curiosity can lead her into trouble.

One sunny morning, Daisy wakes up with a sparkle in her eyes and a spring in her step. Today, she decides she will venture further into the forest than ever before. Her friends, Shaun the squirrel and Rebecca the rabbit, warn her about going too far but Daisy's excitement gets the better of her. She promises herself that she will only explore for a short while and then return home.

With her heart racing, Daisy follows a narrow path that winds deeper and deeper into the forest. The birds sing their sweet melodic tunes and the leaves rustle in the gentle breeze. Daisy is mesmerised by the enchanting beauty surrounding her and kicks the leaves playfully on the ground.

As she wanders along the narrow trail, the sunlight dances through the trees above casting shadows on the ground. The forest is teeming with life and Daisy marvels at the vibrant colours of wildflowers and the gentle rustle of small creatures scurrying about. However, as she strolls deeper into the woods, the joyous symphony of nature suddenly comes to an abrupt halt. Daisy's heart skips a beat when she hears a loud, echoing sound that shatters the tranquility of the forest—a gunshot.

Fear grips her young heart and she instinctively runs and hides behind a nearby tree.

Daisy

Her eyes dart around, searching for the source of the noise. And there, in the distance, she sees a group of hunters dressed in camouflage gear, carrying guns and walking with cautious steps.

Daisy's mind races with confusion and concern, she has heard stories about hunters and how dangerous they are and can't understand why anyone would bring guns into this peaceful forest. Every creature is a treasured part of the delicate balance of the forest and to harm any of them is very bad.

She holds her breath and slowly walks backwards trying her best not to make any noise and alert the hunters. Suddenly there is a loud snap as she steps on a fallen branch and the hunters turn to look at her. Panicked she runs for her life as the sound of their foot steps get closer and closer.

She must have been running for a very long time because when she finally stops she can't hear the hunters anymore but she also doesn't know where she is. She hasn't come this far into the forest before, the once-familiar trees now seem unfamiliar and the path she had been following has now vanished. She calls out for help but there is no response only the echo of her own voice. Tears well up in her eyes as she realises that she is truly lost and scared. Fearful and alone, Daisy doesn't know what to do.

Panic sets in, she feels her little heart pounding as she realises she isn't able to find her way home and may not see her friends or family again.

Just as she is about to give up hope, she hears a soft voice coming from above. She looks up and sees Leila flying up ahead.

"Hello, little one," says Leila, who just happened to be flying by.

"Are you lost?"

Daisy sniffles and nods her head.

Daisy

"Yes, Leila, I am. I went too far into the forest, and was nearly shot at by hunters so I ran and now I don't know how to find my way back home."

Leila scratches her head and has a good look around. She knows this forest well but it is so big even she doesn't know every bit of it or indeed, where Daisy lives.

"Do not worry, young one. I will help you find your way home. First, we must remain calm and think clearly."

Leila explains to Daisy that the forest has many landmarks and clues that will guide them back to where she lives. They search for moss on the side of the trees, which means it is facing north because the sun is usually on the south side. It is also starting to get a little dark now so Leila asks:

"Can you remember where you see the sun in the late evening when you are at home?

"It is normally over there," points Daisy.

"Well, the sun rises in the east and sets in the west so we need to head in that direction," instructs Leila already flying off.

They also listen for the sound of a nearby stream, knowing that water always flows downhill and Daisy remembers climbing up a hill when she was running away from the hunters.

"Is there water near your home?" Leila asks.

"Yes, I live by a river where my family drink and wash," says Daisy.

"Well, it must be this way," commands Leila, following a stream that will lead them to a river. Slowly, Daisy begins to feel a glimmer of hope as

Magical Forest

Leila's confidence and knowledge eases her fears.

As they journey through the forest, Daisy and Leila encounter friendly animals who offer them direction and encouragement. Finally, after what seems like an eternity, Daisy spots a familiar clearing ahead. Her heart soars with joy as she sees her friends Shaun the squirrel and Rebecca the rabbit who have come to look for her. Shaun scurries ahead, showing them a familiar path. Rebecca the rabbit hops alongside, cheering Daisy on with every step. Eventually they reach her home and she sees her family waiting anxiously for her. Daisy runs towards them, feeling relieved and grateful.

Daisy thanks Leila who didn't have to use any of her magic, just her common sense. Leila waves goodbye and wishes Daisy well before flying off back to her village.

From that day forward, Daisy learned a lesson about the importance of staying close to loved ones and not venturing too far without supervision. She realises that even though exploring can be exciting, it is important to remember your way back home and let somebody know where you are going.

Shaun and Rebecca

And so, Daisy, Shaun and Rebecca played happily in the forest, appreciating each other's company. They all understood that true adventure is best shared with friends and family, making memories that will last a lifetime.

CHAPTER 3

Horrible Henry

Leila is friends with all the animals in the forest and she sometimes spends her free time chatting and playing with them. Harry the hedgehog, Barry the badger and Felicity the Fox are some of her closest animal friends.

When it is time for her to go to work they sometimes help her spread joy and happiness throughout the forest. She is loved by all who know her and her magic can bring light to even the darkest of days for most children. However some children were a little harder to help than others, as was the case when she met a boy named Henry. Usually fairies only help children that are pure of heart but Leila always liked a challenge so decided to try and turn this boy around.

Henry was known to be a very bad boy who didn't believed in anything good, especially not in fairies. Some of the other fairies had visited him in the past and tried to guide him but they soon returned to the fairy village distressed and frustrated saying he was beyond help. He is always horrible to everybody he meets and because of that he doesn't have any real friends. His garden is over grown and unkempt as nothing wants to live or grow there. Even the bees and the butterflies refused to go there for fear of being caught by him and having their wings removed. Despite being warned by his parents and teachers, he never listens to them, instead he skips school and spends his time doing things he isn't supposed to do. Henry thinks he is the smartest child in town and nobody can tell him what to do so he spends most of his time alone.

One day when Henry is sat in his overgrown garden picking his nose and flicking it as far as he can, Leila decides to pay him a visit.

Leila

"Hello Henry," she says, surprising him a little, but because Henry doesn't believe in fairies he isn't able to see her and thinks it is just his imagination playing tricks on him. Leila doesn't give up so easily and uses her magic to make herself appear.

Shocked and confused Henry picks up a stone and throws it at her.

"Now you stop that this minute," she insist.

"Or else, what are you going to do?" he asks, taunting her.

"Well, if you don't behave, I will freeze you so you have to listen to what I have to say," she says.

Henry totally ignores her instructions and continues to throw stones at her.

"Well, I did warn you," she says, before waving her magic wand and freezing Henry mid throw.

"Right young Henry Maximus Trotter," she says, calling him by his full name which he doesn't like but can't say or do anything about it because he is frozen under Leila's spell.

"Why are you so mean to everybody? don't you realise that if you carry on doing what you are doing, when you grow up you will be a sad and lonely man?" Still Henry is unable to respond but moves his eyes to show he is listening.

"Now I am going to release you from this spell but if you misbehave again I will re-cast the spell," she warns. Henry shakes his shoulder and exercises his jaw feeling relieved that he can move again.

"Ok then, tell me what the matter is and why you are so mean?" asks Leila.

Henry first shrugs his shoulders but Leila can see that he is just putting on a front so asks him again gently. All of a suddenly he bust into tears for the first time ever and feels the relief at being able to let out his emotions.

Henry

"Well, my father died when I was a baby so I didn't get the chance to know him or kick a ball in the park with him like all the other children do with their dads. I hate school, it is so hard and makes me feel stupid which is why I skip it so much. I am mean to everybody to stop them being mean to me first because nobody likes me," he says, wiping away the tears from his eyes.

Leila is saddened by Henry's words but she know's that she has to do something to help him.

Leila explains to him that sometimes bad things happen to good people and you have to try and appreciate the good things in life. People, like his loving mother and his teachers at school are only trying to help him but if he doesn't listen to them, they will stop trying to help and things will not get better.

"What if I were to tell you that life can be a wonderful thing and there is a lot more to this world than you can imagine?"

"What do you mean?" he asks, a little intrigued.

"Well, you can continue what you are doing and be sad and lonely for the rest of your life or you can come with me and I will show you some of the wonders that exist and how being happy and having friends is amazing."

"Go on then," he says, "show me what you've got."

Leila cast a spell on him and in an instant Henry is transported to a world of magic and wonder in the forest where she lives.

In this new world Henry meets other fairies and creatures he never knew existed. He is amazed by the beauty and kindness of this world and slowly, he begins to change.

"Morning," says a happy frog skipping along the waters edge. Henry mouths morning back before realising he is actually talking to a frog. Other fairies and pixies fly past him smiling and sprinkling fairy dust as they go.

"Mind where you're going!" says a mole, popping its head out from a hole under Henry's feet.

"Sorry," says Henry, stepping over the hole.

"Don't mind her, that's Molly, she is always popping up when you least expect it," says Leila laughing.

Magical Village

Some music is being played in the distance so they head over to see what is going on. A group of pixies are dancing around a tree where soothing beautiful music is being played by a centipede on a home made guitar with at least 100 strings.

"Wow! This is amazing," smiles Henry, looking around and taking in all the wonders of this world.

"I get it now," he says, enjoying the feeling of happiness and seeing lots of people and creatures happily getting along together without hate, fear or discrimination.

"I'm sorry," he says, looking at Leila.

"You don't have to apologise to me, you should apologise to all your friends and family that you have been mean to over the years. And if you find yourself lonely or missing somebody to talk to, just call out my name and I will be there for you. I can't replace your father or kick a ball with you but I am a very good listener and my jokes are not half bad," she smiles.

"Yes I will," he promises and when he returns to the real world he is a totally different person which shocks everybody who ever knew him.

Henry

He helps his mum with the chores, his brother with his homework and the teachers at school handing out books. They can't believe his transformation and when he tries to explain that he talked to a fairy and went to fairy land, they smile patronisingly but don't want to question it incase he returns to his former self.

CHAPTER 4

Mischievous Malice

Today started off as a good day for Leila, the sun was out, the sky was blue and she had helped lots of children. She now has a little time to hang out with some of the other fairies in the village. Most of them are great but there is one fairy named Malice that isn't always the best person to hang out with. Malice is the same age as Leila but has short red hair that sometimes looks like flames in the sunlight. She has a cheeky mischievous smile that draws people in, making it easy for her to fool them. Unlike the other fairies who spread happiness and joy wherever they go, Malice is known to be a mischievous fairy who likes to play tricks and pranks on people and cause chaos. Her tricks range from simple practical jokes to elaborate schemes that leave her victims confused and frustrated. She sometimes sneaks into people's homes and hides their belongings, causes their milk to spoil and makes their flowers wither at the bottom of their gardens, just for fun.

Malice

She also spreads rumours about people causing them to fall out with each other. Once she put washing up liquid in the local stream causing the whole village to fill up with soap suds which took days to clear.

People in the fairy village know to be cautious whenever they hear the fluttering of her wings as they don't know what she will do next.

Malice wasn't always like this, she used to be a good fairy but when the children she helped grew up and stopped believing in her she felt abandoned and alone.

"Those pesky ungrateful children," she would call them, not appreciating that when a child doesn't need you anymore, it means you have done your job well.

Leila has tried to befriend her and guide her in the right direction but her efforts are always in vein.

"Why should i listen to Miss goody two shoes?" she mocks.

The other fairies avoid Malice as much as possible but she doesn't care. She is having too much fun causing chaos and wreaking havoc.

One day Malice goes too far and cast a spell that destroys the mystical cloak protecting the village. She only wanted see what would happen but wasn't able to put it back and it allowed all the bad mythical creatures like trolls, dragons and monsters to enter the village. Luca and his army of Centaurs battled for days with the uninvited creatures until Leila could come up with a spell to replace the mystical curtain.

All the villagers were terrified and some had to run for their lives as the monstrous creatures tried to take over the village.

Mythical Creature

Eventually the battle was won by Luca and his army and Leila managed to repair the curtain and banish the creatures back to where they came from. King Jamie and Queen Melissa of the fairy village were not very happy that their village was put in such danger and arrested Malice. After a short trial they decide to banish Malice from the village until she can prove that she had changed her ways.

Malice is devastated as she never meant to hurt anyone but she had let her mischievous nature get the best of her.

She wanders the wilderness alone, trying to find a way to make things right. Scared and lonely she has time to think about the mischievous things she has done and truly regrets her actions.

One day, she comes across a family who were camping in the forest but got lost. They have been walking around in circles for hours trying to find their way out but it is now getting dark and they are very tired. The man and his wife had wanted to take their only son Jason on this camping adventure so they could spend some quality time together as a family but Jason didn't really want to go. He hated camping and wasn't very happy that he couldn't bring his phone.

"I told you this would be rubbish," says Jason angrily

"It will be fine, we can camp out here another night and try and find our way out in the morning," says the dad, trying to comfort himself as well as his family. They are all very cold, hungry, afraid and it is now also starting to rain. The family all huddle up under a tree and try to keep themselves warm until morning but the rain still manages to get to them. Malice had been listening to them and can hear the fear in their voices.

The man and his wife can't see Malice but Jason can.

Malice

"Don't worry young man, I will help you find your way home," she says.

Jason is a little shocked to see a fairy but also excited as he plays lots of video games and this boring camping trip has now turned very exciting.

"Who are you and where have you come from?" Asks Jason.

"My name is Malice and I am going to help you get home safely," she says with a smile.

She first uses her magic to get the branches of the tree to bend down, creating a canopy over them to shelter them from the rain. She then flys around the forest gathering some safe fruit and nuts for them to eat knowing which ones can be poisonous. She places the food under a nearby tree telling Jason where to find them. She then sprinkles fairy dust on the ground that illuminates in the dark making a sparkling path on the forest floor that will lead them out of the forest to safety.

"Dad, mum, it's going to be alright," says Jason, giving them the fruit and nuts.

"Where did you get all this?" asks his dad surprised.

Fairy Dust Path

"Never mind that, follow me," says Jason showing them Malice's fairy dust path and leading them all out of the forest to safety.

"Thank you," says Jason, waving back at Malice. Malice feels a sense of pride and purpose again and she realises that her mischievous nature didn't have to be a curse, it could be a gift if she uses it wisely.

Family

The family finally make it home and Jason spreads the word to all that will listen about how a fairy called Malice saved their lives. Word of Malices help soon gets to the fairy village and King Jamie and Queen Melissa send their son Luca with a party of centaurs to bring her back. Malice apologises to the King and Queen and all the people she has ever played a prank on including Leila. The King and Queen accept her apology and welcome her back into the village with open arms. Malice promises to use her powers for good from now on and up to this day she has kept her word. She is now known as one of the kindest fairies in the forest and her mischievous ways have become a thing of the past.

CHAPTER 5

Pixie Pete

Leila is now getting older and her parents King Jamie and Queen Melissa are encouraging her to find a nice Prince that she would like to marry one day. Leila isn't really interested in boys, especially the fairy boys that her mother and father are always inviting over to meet her. Most of them are stupid and have no idea about mother nature or the planet which she loves. All they are interested in is playing games and fighting.

There is one boy though that she likes called Pete but not in that way, as a BFF (Best Friend Forever). He really understands her like no other boy ever does and sometimes they just sit on a toadstool in the forest and talk for hours. He makes her laugh a lot and never judges her no matter what she says or does. The only problem is that Pete is a pixie and fairies and pixies are not really supposed to mix, especially as she is a fairy Princess. In the village fairies are the rulers and pixies are the manual workers who look after the village.

Pete

Pete is unlike any other pixie Leila has ever met. His eyes sparkled with charisma and his smile is so contagious it always makes her smile. She can't help but feel drawn to him, despite the fact that their friendship is forbidden. Pixies and fairies have lived together for centuries but they tend to stick to their respective communities and shouldn't hang out with each other socially.

Leila and Pete can't help themselves, they sometimes meet in the hollow of an old oak tree, where the roots twist and turn into a heart shaped nook and they can talk in private and look up at the sky.
They usually sit for hours, sometimes until the sun sets in the sky and time seems to run away.

Nook

They share stories and secrets about their lives and each day their friendship grows stronger and stronger. However, when Leila's father, the King, finds out about their secret friendship and forbids her from ever seeing Pete again. Leila is devastated and determined to be with her BFF so she and Pete hatch a plan to run away together.

One night, under the cover of darkness, they flee the village, leaving their homes and their communities behind. They journey across vast landscapes, facing danger and adversity at every turn but they never lose sight of their friendship.

Finally, after what feels like an eternity, they find a quiet corner of the forest where they can be together without fear of judgment or persecution. Unfortunately, the place they find is inhabited by a wicked witch.

The witch was once a fairy herself but hundreds of years ago she was cast out of the village because she used her magic for evil and created black magic spells to harm others for her own gain. Over the years her black magic has started to deform her giving her a croaked nose, black teeth and boils all over her face.

Witch

She has longed to capture a fairy for years to reap revenge on them for banishing her and to steal their beauty for herself. When she sees Leila and Pete approaching, she hides behind a tree and when they are close enough, she cast one of her dark spells on them.

The spell puts Leila into a deep sleep so she can't use

her fairy magic and paralyses Pete so he can't move or

fly away. She then gets her evil helpers, a black cat and

a toothless bat to help her get them to her lair and lock

them up in a cage.

Bat

The only way for Pete to rescue Leila from her deep sleep and break the witches spell is to find a rare herb that grows in the forest. He has heard people in the village speak of the herb before but if he can't escape, he can't get the herb and even if he does escape, he has no idea where to look for it.

"I will soon have your beauty and your magic," boasts the witch as she stirs her cauldron and chants a spell. The smell of her potion is so bad it makes her cough and fart at the same time.

"Excuse me," she says as the cat runs out of the kitchen and into the fresh air outside. The smell slowly makes its way over to Pete who wants to defend himself by holding his nose but he is paralysed and can't move.

"Let us out," he shouts, nearly passing out from the combination of fart and potion.

"And why would I want to do that?" she laughs. Pete has no reply except, "because I said so."

"Once I get your little friends powers, I don't need you anymore," chortles the witch letting out another fart but this time it is silent so catches Pete off guard. When it does reach him he wished he was put to sleep like Leila.

"You are disgusting," he shouts, but the witch just ignores him and carries on with her cooking.
Pete needs a plan and quick, before the witch can finish her potion and take away Leila's magic.

"Your beauty will always be there no matter what she does to you," he says to Leila as she lies there peacefully in a deep sleep.

Pete is now getting very scared because he doesn't know what to do. As he sits there thinking of ways to escape, he notices a tiny mouse scurrying across the ground. The mouse stops in front of him and looks up with big, curious eyes.

"Can you help us escape?" he asks, in a quiet voice so the witch doesn't hear.

The mouse thinks for a moment then remembers how much the witches cat had tormented him over the years.

"Yes I will help," he says, nodding his head. "What do you need?"

"There is a rare herb called Ashwagandha which grows in the forest somewhere. If you can find it and bring it back to me, it will un-paralyse me and wake up Princess Leila so we can escape," he instructs.

The mouse thinks for a while.

"I am not sure where to find the herb, but I know somebody who will," he says, scurrying away, through the tunnels and passages of the witches' lair, and making his way to a hidden alcove where a wise old owl is perched on a branch.

"Hello Mike," says the owl as the mouse approaches.

"What can I do for you?" he asks.

"Hi Ollie, we need your help to rescue the fairy Princess from the witches spell," says the mouse, out of breath from running.

Ollie

"Fairy Princess," the owl repeats, "do you mean Leila?" he asks concerned.

"Yes, Leila and Pete the pixie have been captured by the witch and they need our help.

"Of coarse I will can help you, I know Leila well," says the owl, turning his head 360 degrees while he thinks about what to do.

"Pete said if we can find a rare herb called Ashwag.. ashwigan.."

"You mean Ashwagandha," says the owl.

"Yes, that's it," says the mouse.

"Right, it can be found by the riverbank under the rickety bridge. You must be careful because a miserable crocodile lives there. You then need to mix the herb with water from the river to make the anti potion. Let me know when you get back and I will create a distraction so you can give it to Pete," orders the owl.

The mouse heads off to the riverbank and is just about to pick some of the herb when he is suddenly confronted by the crocodile.

"What are you doing here?" Croaks the crocodile. Mike the mouse freezes with fear as the green eyes of the crocodile look right through him.

Mike

"I'm sorry," squeaks Mike eventually. "I was just getting some of this herb to rescue the Princess," he continues preparing himself to be eaten.

"Do you mean Princess Leila?" asks the crocodile.

"Yes, Leila has been captured by the witch," explains Mike, still feeling the crocodiles breath on his neck.

"Well, help yourself," urges the crocodile. Shocked, Mike hurriedly collects the herbs and quietly tries to tip toe away.

"Oy," Croaks the crocodile. Mike freezes again, thinking the crocodile has changed his mind and is going to eat him.

"Good luck," he says before slithering back into the murky depths of the river.

"Thank you," says Mike already scurrying off, wondering how Leila knows so many animals. When he returns, the owl puts his plan in to action.

"Whoooo, whooooo, whooooo," hoots the owl loudly, flapping his wings and creating a commotion outside the witches' lair.

"Whatever can that be?" asks the witch looking out her dirty window. She can't see much so she goes outside to investigate. As she opens the door, the mouse sneaks in under her feet and gives Pete the potion he made with the herbs. Pete drinks the potion and can instantly move again. He gently lifts Leila's head and slowly drip feeds the medicine on to her lips. Pete is becoming a little worried as nothing seems to be happening.

"Give her some more," instructs the mouse,"
Pete slowly pours a little more into her mouth and after a few minutes, Leila starts to wake up.

"What happened, where am I?" she ask, still a little groggy from the spell.

"We are trapped in the witches lair but we have to move quick, before she comes back," he explains.

"Leave this to me," says Leila.

"Bibidy bobidy boo," she says, waving her wand and breaking open the cage door.

With the mouse leading the way, Leila and Pete run out of the witches' lair. Outside the cat is lying in wait but the mouse has already set a plan to take care of him.

Before he entered the witches lair to give Pete the potion he saw the cat sleeping outside. Slowly and quietly he snook up behind the cat and tied its tail to a tree with some string.

Witches Cat

When the cat sees them he tries to run and tell the witch but the string pulls him back. The Mouse taunts the cat and sticks out its tongue before following Leila and Pete into the forest.

Once they are safely out of the witches reach, they stop to catch their breath. Leila thanks Mike and Olly the owl.

"Thank you so much for your help," she says. Olly the owl smiles and gives them wise words.

"Remember Leila, even the smallest of creatures can make a big difference."
Leila then thanks Pete for being so brave and coming up with a plan to save them both.

"I would do anything for you, my BFF," he says kissing her on her cheek.

They both make their way back to their fairy village tired and hungry from an eventful night and a long journey back. Leila apologises to her parents the King and Queen who have already sent out Luca with some of his bravest soldiers to find her.

Queen Melissa

"We are just happy to have you back safe and sound," says the Queen giving Leila a hug.

"And for you young man," says the King in a deep stern voice. Pete is afraid he is going to be imprisoned or even worst, banished from the village.

"The Queen and I would like to thank you for bringing our little girl back to us. I admirer your bravery and understand that you must really be a good friend to our daughter to risk running away with her. Myself and the leader of the pixies have had a discussion and we feel that there should be no discrimination about who you are friends with. We all need to live together peacefully and happily no matter who or what you are."

After the Kings speech the whole village of fairies and pixies cheer and the King and Queen put on a celebration for everybody, organised by the pixies who know how to throw a good party.

And so, the forbidden friendship of a pixie and a fairy Princess flourished, defying the odds and proving that true friendship knows no bounds.

CHAPTER 6

Save the Forest

L eila is woken up suddenly by loud crashing noises and the ground shaking beneath her feet. Hanging pictures fall to the floor shattering the glass in their frames, spilling photographs of good times. Panicked and confused, she shoots out of bed and runs out into the village to see what is going on. Lots of other fairies, pixies and magical creatures have also left their homes and are now gathered in the village square looking for answers from the King and Queen.

"What's happening, is it an earth quake?" they ask, as the ground begins to shake again beneath their feet.

"Everybody remain calm," commands King Jamie, slightly panicked himself but taking control. Lois clings onto her big sisters leg while baby Luna cries in her mothers arms.

"Shall I go and see what is going on?" asks Leila.

"No," says the King, "it is not a job for a Princess, your brother can go," he says dismissively.

"Luca, Luca," he calls, but there is no answer.

" Luca," he shouts louder as his first inline to the throne son emerges half dressed and half asleep.

"What is it, what's all the fuss about," he asks, rubbing the sleep from his eyes.

"Why were you still in bed, did you not hear the commotion?" Jamie asks.

"Sorry dad, I had a late night," says Luca yawning.

"Well wake up and take your bravest centaurs and go and see what is happening," he commands.

This all seems to be taking too long for Leila so she gathers some of her animal friends and because she knows the forest like the back of her hand, takes a short cut to where the noises are coming from.

As they get closer the noises become so loud Leila has to cover her sensitive ears. As they round a corner they see men in the forest with diggers and chain saws cutting down trees and digging up the luscious green grass that has carpeted and sheltered the forest for hundreds of years. A single tear falls from Leila's eyes as she sees the local animals that live there running for their lives, some with their young following behind.

Workman

The big oak tree that she used to play on when she was a young girl now lays horizontal on the ground. She can hear the men talking about clearing the forest to make room for a big block of houses and a carpark. If that happens the animals and the fairies who live here will have nowhere to go.

"What are we going to do?" asks Barry the badger, worriedly.

Leila thinks hard and eventually comes up with a plan.

"Right, you guys stay here and stall the workers until my brother gets here and I will be back as soon as I can," she instructs before flying off back through the forest.

"Right, you heard her," says Berti the bee to the rest of the animals and they all descend on the workers. The bees get together and swarm around the man in the digger truck making him jump out and run for his life as he is scared of getting stung. Molly the mole and her friends pop in and out of the ground under the feet of the workers so they don't know where to step and Shaun and his squirrel friends scurry up and down the trees throwing nuts and berries at their helmets.

"What's going on?" ask the foreman as the workers start to leave the site.

"The forest has gone mad," says one of the workers scratching his head in disbelief.

"I'm not working in these conditions," says another worker.

"Alright, everybody, calm down and take the day off, I will get a team of pest controllers out tomorrow to get rid of these pesky animals."

As the workers start to leave, Luca turns up with his army of centaurs too late as always.

"Yeah, you had better leave," he shouts to the back of their heads but they can't hear him for the sound of theirs trucks driving away.

Meanwhile Leila has her own mission, she sometimes revisits people that she has helped when they were children. Mainly out of curiosity to see how they have grown up but also to check to see that they are ok. She remembers visiting Sarah one day who is now in her twenties and that she said she was going to work for a company that has something to do with protecting the environment. The only problem is Sarah doesn't need fairies anymore so she won't be able to see or hear her. Leila needs help to make her plan work so she goes to see Malice on her way over.

"Now Malice I know I told you that being mischievous was wrong but I need you to forget all that and help me with this one task."

Leila explains the situation to her and although a little confused, Malice agrees to help.

Malice

It started off as just a normal day for Sarah, she got out of bed, brushed her teeth and had her breakfast before heading into her office. That is when the day first started to get a little strange. She remembers hanging up her coat when she arrived but when she looks around it is on the floor. She hangs it up again and goes to the bathroom but when she comes back, there it is again, on the floor. Somebody at work must be playing a joke on me she thinks and puts her coat on the back of the chair this time. Next, the door to her office that she closed before she sat down is now open. She gets up and shuts it again, checking the windows to see if there is a draught but there isn't as it is a beautiful sunny day. As she goes to sit down, the door opens by itself again.

Something very strange is going on she thinks but decides to shake it off and carry on with her work.

When she goes to use her pen it starts moving on its own across her desk.

Sarah

She reaches for it but it moves away further and starts to stand itself up and move towards a piece of paper.

Sarah stands up in shock and looks around the office to see if anybody else can see what is happening but they are all engrossed in their work. The pen now starts to write something on the paper in big capital letters. Sarah watches in disbelief as it spells out the word H.E.L.P. and then the word L.E.I.L.A. Suddenly she starts to remember her childhood and the fairy she used to talk to at the bottom of her garden and how she helped her find her favourite doll. As she continues to remember, Leila and Malice slowly start to appear in front of her.

"Sarah, sorry for the intrusion but we really need your help," Leila says. Sarah is still slightly in shock but starts to come round as her memories get stronger.

"Is this real, are you real," she asks looking around her office to see if anybody else is witnessing two fairies sat on her desk in her office, but again everybody else is oblivious.

Leila

"Yes we are real, this is Malice who helped me to do all the mischievous things to get your attention."

"Hi Malice and Leila, I haven't thought about you in years, I thought you were just a figment of my imagination when I was a child."

"We only show up when children need us and disappear when they don't or they stop believing in fairies. But this time we need your help."

"What can I do," asks Sarah now fully believing again.

"Well, the forest and our magical kingdom is being torn down as we speak by some workmen and we want you to help us stop them. If they tear down the forest then the animals will have nowhere to live and the rest of the fairies and pixies will have to move on but we love that forest and don't want to go."

"Right, leave it to me, I also love that forest so I will put a halt to the demolition work and look into it," she says. Leila and Malice fly back to the forest to tell the others who had already stopped the workers for today but they said they will be back tomorrow. The following day the workers are back and this time they have a whole team of animal control experts with nets and sprays trying to catch the animals and spray the bugs who are also helping to stop the work. Leila waits patiently to hear from Sarah and true to her word, she manages to get an injunction to stop the work until an investigation can take place.

"Hey, you, stop what you are doing?" she shouts from a distance waving the injunction in the air.

"Who are you?" asks the foreman confused.

"I'm the one who will sue you if you don't stop what you are doing now and call off all your workmen." The man angrily grabs the piece of paper and reads it before throwing it back at her and calling his men off.

"You haven't heard the last of this, we'll be back." he says before his team start their engines and drive off. The whole forest applaud and cheer as the last of the trucks disappears into the distance.

"This is only a temporary injunction guys so don't build your hopes up too much, I now have to build a case as to why this forest should remain open and take it to court." The cheering slows down as they realise this is only the start of their fight.

Sarah gets to work straight away putting all her other work to one side and concentrates on saving the forest. Leila visits her regularly to help with her case and to keep the King and Queen informed of progress.

Eventually the case goes to court and the building company arrive with their lawyers in flashy cars and expensive suits. Sarah arrives in her blue and white VW Beatle car and parks proudly next to them. The building company states their case to the judge saying that the area is in need of more housing for the people and that the forest is a useless piece of land that serves no purpose. Sarah takes to the stand.

"Your honour, I grew up going to the forest as a child like half of the people who live in this town. It has always been a magical place that I and all the children who have grown up near the forest have enjoyed. This useless piece of land as the builders put it, houses an array of different animals including badgers, foxes, rabbits, hedgehogs and squirrels. If the forest was to be torn down then these animals would have nowhere to go plus the magic of the forest would be lost to all children forever.

Courtroom

Your honour, not only are the beautiful trees been cut down, hunters have been seen shooting at the animals who live there peacefully."

The jury, many of whom had grown up in the town applauded Sarah when she finishes and the judge has to shout out the words "Order in the court," to calm them down.

Outside the court something else going on. Some of the animals from the forest have travelled to the court room to show their support. Daisy the deer cheers loudly when Sarah mentions the hunters. Most of the animals are outside looking through the window but some of the little ones have managed to sneak into the court.

Because of the commotion, the TV and news channels have taken an interest in the story and are outside the court room interviewing people.

"So Sir, what is your name and what do you think about saving the forest?" asks the reported.

"Hello, my name is Henry Trotter and I grew up near the forest and loved seeing the animals running about freely. It always had a magical feeling and I might have dreamt it but I vaguely remember being helped by a fairy once at the bottom of my garden," says Henry who is now grown up with a young family of his own. The reporter looks at him a little strange before continuing her report to the camera.

"As you can see, people and animals a like seem to love this forest so let's wait and see what the judge says."

Leila and Malice are at the back of the court room watching with bated breath as the case continues. The other animals make their presence known by running around the building. Some mice make people scream as they run around their feet in the court room. The judge bangs down his hammer again and shouts, "Order!" as the jury and the spectators witness the array of animals outside and inside the court.

"Quiet in the court," he instructs. "This is all a little strange I know but I can't help thinking that having all these animals around is an omen. I also played in the forest as a child and felt its magical

powers,"

"But your honour, there is no such thing as

magical powers," interrupts the prosecution.

Judge

"And do you have any proof of that statement?"

asks the judge.

"Well no, but there is no proof that it does exist," replies the prosecution.

"Then we are at a stalemate, because it's only true if you believe it is and I for one do not want to take away the belief from children if as you say you can't prove it doesn't exist. The forest may not be a home for people but as the defence so eloquently put it, it is a home for hundreds of species of animals as well as other things.

"What do you mean, other things?" Ask the prosecution.

"Like I said, you never know what may lie deep in the forest as it is and will remain a mystical place," says the judge staring right into Leila's eyes.

"Did he just look at you?" asks Malice, who is standing next to her.

"I'm not sure, I think he can see us," says Leila.

"Watch this," Malice gives the judge a wave and the judge gives her a wink back.

"Oh my god, I think he still believes in us," smiles Leila.

"So in conclusion, I would like all work to cease in the forest immediately and I would like the building company to pay for the trees that have already been cut down to be replanted.

"But judge," pleads the prosecution.

"And from this day, there is to be no hunting in the forest because the animals have a right to live in peace like the rest of us, case dismissed," says the judge slamming his hammer down for the last time. The whole court cheer and the animals celebrate outside dancing and jumping about, especially Daisy the deer.

"Thank you Sarah," says Leila.

"You are welcome, thank you for making my childhood amazing," says Sarah.

"You're welcome," says Leila before flying off back to the forest with the rest of the animals in tow to tell her parents the good news.

When she gets back to the village, news has already reached them and the King gives Leila a big hug while her sister Lois smiles hoping to be like her big sister when she grows up.

"Thank you so much my child, you are forever proving yourself to be a brave and courageous girl.

Your mother and I are not getting any younger and I know Luca is down to becomes the next ruler of the village but if he doesn't buck up his ideas it could be coming to you,"

King Jamie

"But dad," protest Luca.

"Don't worry Bruv, I don't want to be the ruler of the village but we can definitely work together if you want."

"Yes, that sounds good," says Luca relieved giving her a high five but misses. They all laugh and hug each other as Lois looks up to her big sister and baby Luna chortles happily away in his mothers arms.

THE END

In a world that often seeks to confine us within the boundaries of the ordinary, you can choose to look beyond what meets the eye. You should embrace the power of imagination, where dreams are not mere figments of the mind but the whispers of possibility. With wide-eyed innocence, you can embarked on a journey that leads you to realms untouched, where the extraordinary flourishes.

To the young souls who refused to surrender their belief in the fantastical, they are the keepers of wonder. They remind us of the precious gift we carry within us—a sense of awe that knows no limits. Their unwavering faith in the existence of something more gives birth to miracles, breathing life into the mundane and infusing it with enchantment.

Through their dreams, they can teach us that the pursuit of the unknown is not a folly but a courageous act of embracing the limitless potential of the human spirit. It is in those fleeting moments of solitude when imagination dances hand in hand with reality, that we catch glimpses of what could be. The barriers that bind us crumble and we are free to explore the uncharted territories of our hearts and minds.

This dedication is a celebration of the daring dreamers, who have dared to push the boundaries of the ordinary. Your spirits shine bright like stars in the night sky, guiding us towards new horizons. You remind us that the impossible is merely a challenge, an invitation to step outside our comfort zones and venture into the realm of the extraordinary.

May you forever hold on to the innocence that fuels your imagination. In a world that often scoffs at the magical and the unknown, you are the guardians of possibility. Cherish the dreams that dance within your hearts, for they are the blueprints of a future yet to be revealed.